dick bruna

miffy's
birthday

EGMONT

Little Miffy one fine day

was early out of bed

she washed herself from top to toe

there now, that's done, she said.

Then from her cupboard Miffy took

her very prettiest dress

but why? it was her birthday, so

she liked to look her best.

Then in came Miffy's mum and dad

happy returns! said they

and Miff said, thank you very much

this is a lovely day.

Oh look, you've made my chair look sweet

with flowers, just like my dress

with yellow hearts and little leaves

however did you guess?

And what about those parcels there

are they all meant for me?

I must unwrap them straight away

oh, I can't wait to see.

Some scissors first that really cut

a lovely whistle too

and coloured crayons, oh hurrah!

red, yellow, green and blue.

Then in the afternoon her friends

Aggie and Win came by

a happy birthday, Miff, they said

and Miffy felt quite shy.

What fun they had, the three of them

they played some lovely games

and threw a shiny ball about

until the evening came.

And in the evening Grandpa Bun

and Grandma came to tea

and they had brought a parcel, too

whatever could it be?

A bear, a woolly teddy bear

so cuddly, soft and bright

I'll take him with me, Miffy cried

up to my bed tonight.

They had a real dinner then

Miffy at Grandpa's side

and Teddy sat on Miffy's lap

which filled the bear with pride.

When Miffy's mother late that night

took Miff and Ted to bed

oh thank you for a happy day

my birthday, Miffy said.

miffy's library

miffy
miffy's dream
miffy goes to stay
miffy is crying
miffy at the seaside
miffy at school

miffy at the playground
miffy in hospital
miffy's bicycle
miffy at the gallery
miffy's birthday
miffy the fairy

miffy's garden
miffy and the new baby
dear grandma bunny
miffy at the zoo

"het feest van nijntje"
First published in Great Britain 1997 by Egmont UK Limited
239 Kensington High Street, London W8 6SA.
Publication licensed by Mercis Publishing bv, Amsterdam
Original text Dick Bruna © copyright Mercis Publishing bv, 1970
Illustrations Dick Bruna © copyright Mercis bv, 1970
Original English translation © copyright Patricia Crampton, 1995
The moral right of the author has been asserted.
Printed in China
ISBN 978 1 4052 1023 2
10 9 8 7 6 5 4 3